THE HERO CLUB

52 Weekly Stories

to Share with Your Children about Courage, Compassion, Honesty and other Character Traits that will Inspire Kids to be Heroes

By Ferah Ozbek

Illustrations by Oleg Kravets

Publishing services and cover design provided by:

ISBN-13: 978-1545317747

A FREE GIFT FOR YOU!

You can download all 53 color illustrations for each chapter of *The Hero Club*. You can tack the chapter's illustration on your refrigerator with a magnet as you read and discuss each story. The illustrations will be a good way to remind your child about the character trait discussed in the stories and will be a fun way to engage your child in conversations during dinner and throughout the week. To download your free illustrations, go to my website: ferahozbek.com/hero

DEDICATION

I dedicate this book to my two beloved sons. This is the book I have wanted to write for you for many years. I want you to start your journey with the most important character trait, courage.

Courage means doing the right thing no matter what the consequences. That is, do you stand out in the face of adversity and do the principled thing, or do you go along with the crowd? The courageous thing is the right thing to do, and you can be courageous and scared at the same time. I hope you will have the courage to intervene on behalf of a stranger who is being mocked or bullied because of his or her race, religion, or ethnicity. I hope you have the courage to argue a viewpoint that you believe is right, even if it is not popular.

In Harper Lee's book *To Kill a Mockingbird*, her central figure was the lawyer Atticus Finch. For many lawyers, Atticus is an inspiration and a true hero. He is deeply principled, honest, and a tireless crusader for justice. He teaches his daughter, Scout, many things, including not to judge others. Atticus says to Scout, "If you can learn a simple trick, Scout, you'll get along a lot better with all kinds of folks. You never really understand a person until you consider things from his point of view … until you climb into his skin and walk around in it." I hope you will have the courage to respond to an intolerant person by defending the victim of his wrath. Will you have the courage to leave those in your presence who are gossiping or badmouthing others? I hope you won't engage in useless talk, especially talk that speaks badly about others and puts others down.

Sometimes courage just means showing up. You may be frightened by a new experience or to join a new club or take a new class, but you never know if you will like it, love it, or hate it until you try. That takes courage. When you have courage, you try new things, and sometimes you will fail. But failure teaches you new things. The more failures you experience in life, the more courage you develop to try new things. I hope you try new things and fail a lot so you can get up and try more new things and become better all the time.

The difference between winning and losing is how fast you get up after a failure. You may fail, but just get back up and try again. Try something new, try something else, but don't ever wallow in fear or pity. Take action—no matter how scared you may feel, just show up.

I hope that when you feel like quitting you have the courage to go on—whether it is during a sports activity, a course you are taking that may seem difficult at first, or any other endeavor you have embarked upon. Having the courage to take small, incremental steps will let you achieve any task. You just have to take action. Any time you feel like quitting or giving up, just imagine the consequences of that action—try to look down the road, perhaps months or years down the road instead of today or tomorrow or next week. I encourage you to think about your long-term goals and how this task is just one part of your larger goal.

Maya Angelou described courage as the most important of all virtues because without courage you cannot practice any virtue consistently. Martin Luther King said that our lives begin to end the day we become silent about things that really matter.

Aristotle said, "Courage is the first of human qualities because it is the quality which guarantees the others."

My wonderful sons, courage has many forms. Courage can be physical courage or mental courage or moral courage. Courage is not the absence of fear, but taking action despite your fears. I wish for you a life filled with courage; courage to always be true to yourself and courage to do the right thing.

CONTENTS

INTRODUCTION

The best gift you can give your child is good character because the most perfect people are those with the best character.

I've always thought that good character is the main skill children need to thrive in the world. The best way for you to teach character is by your own example. This book is intended as an easy way for you to teach and reinforce character traits that will help you raise children with conscience, empathy, courage, and principle.

I always wanted my children to have courage to do the right thing, to never sit on the sidelines and watch others being bullied, harassed, or treated badly. I shared stories with them of people in history who were principled and had courage to do the right thing, which benefited not only the oppressed but the entire world.

The gift of good character does not cost money, but it will reap rewards that are worth more than any amount of money. The lessons you teach your children will empower them to be respected adults, good citizens, and leaders in a global world. Having good character will allow your child to be guided by conscience and do the right thing for the right reasons. It will enable them to live with integrity. While we teach our children that silence is golden, character will teach them to never be silent when they see suffering or injustice.

On December 10, 1986, in Oslo, Norway, Elie Wiesel—a Holocaust survivor—accepted the Nobel Peace Prize. In response to how the world remained silent when millions were systematically murdered, he said that he tried to keep the memory alive because if we forgot, we were guilty and accomplices when we knew what was happening and remained silent. During his acceptance speech, he humbly and eloquently said: "And that is why I swore never to be silent whenever wherever human beings endure suffering and humiliation. We must take sides. Neutrality helps the oppressor, never the victim. Silence encourages the tormentor, never the tormented. Sometimes we must interfere … One person … one person of integrity can make a difference …"

It is profound to know that people can turn their backs and ignore those who are suffering because they are unaffected by the tormentor and would rather not get involved. I've always thought of a leader as someone who is willing to stand up for their beliefs, do the right things, passionately argue their viewpoints, and make tough choices in the face of adversity or when the right thing is unpopular. And it is my wish that all children are taught the importance of Wiesel's words.

These fifty-two character lessons are stories you can share with your child each week of the year. I purposely chose fifty-two chapters for the fifty-two character traits with the thought that they be used as a weekly lesson for your children. You can use them as conversation subjects during dinner to engage your child about their experiences at school. You can use them to share your own experiences you encountered at work or at home dealing with everyday issues of life. You can use them as a means to have your child open up about events they have encountered at school or with friends, relatives, acquaintances, or strangers.

It is my hope that this book will be an easy-to-use tool to have important conversations with your child in a systematic way—in a way your child will never forget. Hopefully, they will be able to apply these lessons to their lives. As we are all busy in life, sometimes we don't have time to discuss the most important things with our children. While we know these conversations are important, sometimes life just happens. We have the best intentions, but we just don't make time to teach our children the most important concepts that will undoubtedly determine their success and happiness.

I hope this book will serve as a guide for your children when they are at home and, most importantly, when they are far away from home and interacting with the world around them. It is my sincere hope that this book will serve as a reminder about how we should all behave—especially when no one is looking.

As the mother of two pure and energetic boys, I wondered how to teach them how to grow into good human beings, young adults who were sure of themselves. I want them to be confident but also good humans who do their part to make the world a better place. I always thought that if I had a chapter book, I could use one chapter to reinforce a concept throughout the week. I'd tape the character trait for the week on the refrigerator to reinforce the concept and encourage my sons to apply the trait in their daily interactions and experiences.

We are not born with character; it must be taught by example or lessons. You either learn character by observing the actions of your parents, grandparents, or those who raise you or through some formal education (spiritual or otherwise) that teaches you values you have not been exposed to before. Character is a powerful weapon and guide for behavior in bad times, in times of utter frustration, anger, and fear. If you rely on principles, you will persevere through the toughest times with grace and patience.

Heraclitus said that character is destiny. I believe this with all my heart. Your character, your behavior, is how you react to disappointment and bad actions of others toward you. Character is revealed not in times of contentment and happiness but in times of peril.

I hope this book will be a guide to help you and those you love.

The stars of this book are: Andy, Mai, Rob, Hannah, Daniel, and Isabella. Enjoy their stories and the exemplary character they all display. The name "The Hero Club" is dedicated to the characters in this book, as they are my heroes. You will see the children display the best character that we should all aspire to. They are heroes and part of a special club representing children who are heroes all over the world.

These children are all eight-year-olds and third grade students at Lyncrest Elementary School. They are of different backgrounds, religions, and ethnicities, but they are all Americans first. They are children who want to be the best they can be and have learned at an early age the principles of character. And it is their character that guides their decisions and actions each day.

I hope you and your child find their stories inspirational. Remember, someone is always watching and hoping to see inspiring acts—hoping so they can have the courage to be inspiring too.

Best wishes during your journey to a better world for yourself and your loved ones.

MEET THE CHARACTERS

It was a bright September morning, and fall was in the air. Kids bustled about, trying to find their classrooms on the first day of school. The teachers were excited to meet their new students and eager to teach and inspire them as they progressed through elementary school.

Six students were huddled in one corner of the room, talking and introducing themselves. They were nervous and excited to be starting the third grade and happy they were in each other's first class period. Andy, Mai, Rob, Hannah, Daniel, and Isabella were wide-eyed, exchanging stories about what sports they wanted to play in gym this year and their favorite Pokémon characters in Pokémon Go.

They were all students at Lyncrest Elementary and were assigned to Room 122, their homeroom class. Room 122 was the art room. It was filled with paintings and drawings created by students from previous years. The art teacher proudly displayed the artwork to showcase her students' talents.

Andy lived with his father, mother, and little sister. Andy loved to read. His passion was baseball, and his hero was Jackie Robinson. His dad promised to take him to a baseball game in New York City, and he dreamed about the day he would be sitting in the stands and watching his favorite team play while he ate hotdogs and popcorn. Andy wanted to become an astronaut. His father was a retired United States Air Force pilot, and Andy knew that he wanted to fly the fastest airplanes and one day explore space in the fastest rockets.

Mai's grandparents were from China. While her parents did not speak Mandarin because her grandparents wanted their children to learn English, she hoped to learn the language one day and visit the home of her ancestors. Mai loved computers and spent every spare moment playing computer games and trying to learn how to make her own games. Her father bought her a simple book that taught children how to write computer programs, and she spent hours trying to learn how to design a game she could play with her friends.

Rob's grandparents were from Ireland and he wanted to be a lawyer. He loved to play rugby and watch football with his father. His mom always said he was good at persuading her with his arguments. He had seen the movie *To Kill a Mockingbird*, and it made a big impression on him. He wanted to be just like Atticus Finch and fight for justice. Rob had a picture of Atticus Finch in his room.

Hannah's great-grandparents were from Hungary. They were Jewish refugees who had fled during World War II and settled in New York City. Hannah's hero was Albert Einstein. She wanted to be a physicist just like him. Her dad was a physics professor at a university, and she loved to go to classes with him in the summer. There she would sit in the back of the room and watch him write formulas and draw diagrams. Hannah knew that if she worked hard she could be whatever she wanted to become—even the president of the United States.

Daniel's parents were from Bosnia. They came to the United States after the war in Yugoslavia. Daniel dreamed of becoming a doctor because he wanted to help cure his grandfather, who had Alzheimer's and could not speak to Daniel as the disease had destroyed parts of his brain. He dreamed of one day talking to his grandfather and hearing him tell him stories of Bosnia again. Daniel loved science and reading books. His room was filled with books from the library. All of the librarians knew Daniel, as the library was his second home.

Isabella's parents were from Mexico and had come to America for a better life. She loved school and learning, and her dream was to be a teacher. Her mother had bought her a chalkboard, and she loved standing in front of the board and pretending to teach her younger brothers spelling and math. Isabella gave her little brothers treats when they knew the answers to questions she asked. Her eyes lit up when they learned new things she taught them and repeated it back to her perfectly.

The class bell rang, and the students quickly stopped talking, ready to hear what was in store for them that day. They all had a feeling that they would be the best of friends as they were starting their first day of school in the same class together.

CHAPTER 1: COURAGE

When the school bell rang, the students knew it was time for their teacher to begin class. Everyone was in his or her assigned seat. Andy sat next to a boy named David, whom he had spoken to before class started. Andy thought David was very bright. When David spoke, he stuttered somewhat, so his speech was interrupted.

"D—do you I—like math?" David said to Andy.

"Yes, I do," Andy replied.

"So do I. It is my favorite subject," said David.

Andy was not distracted by David's stuttering, and he knew that they would be friends. When the class began, Mr. Wright told them they would be doing a lot of reading in the English class.

"Good morning, class. I'm Mr. Wright, your English teacher. So tell me, who is excited to learn?"

"Meee!" the class chorused.

"I know you all want to learn, but I must inform you that you all need to read in order to learn."

"Mr. Wright, why do we need to read for us to learn?" Grace asked.

"We have to read because it helps us to learn new vocabulary and also helps us to write better," said Mr. Wright.

Mr. Wright wanted everyone to introduce themselves to each other. He had everyone tell the class their name and their favorite subject.

"Edward Brown, Science," said one of the students.

"James Waters. My favorite subject is English," another boy told the class.

When it was David's turn, he said his name, and he began to stutter as he started to say *mathematics*.

"My name is David Johnson, M—ma—a..."

The word would not come out of his mouth. Two boys sitting behind Andy began laughing at David. Andy's ears turned red. He was unhappy that the kids were making fun of David. David finally got the word out, and Mr. Wright went around the room until everyone had introduced himself or herself.

As soon as class was over, Andy turned around and told the two boys behind him that they should not have laughed when David was trying to speak.

Andy said, "It's too bad that you had to embarrass David. I am sure it is hard enough for him to get his words out, but then when you laughed at him, you made it worse."

The boys snickered and began to walk away.

Andy said, "You need to apologize to David."

One boy yelled back, "And what if we don't?"

Andy said that if they didn't, they would lose friends. Not only would David not be their friend, but neither would Andy nor the rest of the class. Andy looked around, and the children in the class were all looking at him. They began clapping and patting both David and Andy on the back. They all shouted, "Yes, that's right! We don't like bullies who make fun of others. So if you want us to be friends with you, you better apologize to David."

"All right, we are sorry," one of the boys said. Then the boys reached out and shook David's hand. David had a big smile on his face and said he was happy they could all be friends.

Andy was happy he had the courage to stand up for David. This was not a surprise because Andy's father was in the United States Air Force and had told him that courage was hard but important.

"Son, always remember to stand up for others." His dad had always told him that, and that's what he did.

CHAPTER 2: COMPASSION

Daniel and Isabella sat next to each other in Mr. Mellner's class. They shared similar backgrounds. While they were born in the United States, their parents had emigrated from other countries. Therefore, they could relate to the struggles their parents faced learning English. Despite their young age, they had to take on responsibilities as translators for their parents, and Daniel had to help care for his grandfather, who had Alzheimer's.

Isabella was a born leader. She loved to teach her younger brothers things she learned at school. "I want to be the best teacher," Isabella would say. Daniel and Isabella were both very compassionate and liked to help their classmates.

One day as Daniel and Isabella were walking to school, they saw a homeless man.

"Isabella, do you see that man? I think he needs help," Daniel said with sadness in his voice.

"Yes, Daniel, let's help him. He looks hungry. We can give him our lunch."

Isabella opened her schoolbag, reached for her peanut butter and jelly sandwich, and handed it to the man. Daniel reached for his apple and gently placed it in the man's hand.

"This is all we have, sir. We hope you will like it," said Isabella.

They knew that being compassionate meant that you take others' feelings into consideration, not only your own feelings. They knew that being compassionate did not only mean helping others with food or money, but also using skills or knowledge like when Mai and Hannah helped their friends with math problems. Being compassionate might also mean helping an elderly woman or man cross the street.

Daniel and Isabella were happy to help a person in need. Their acts of kindness brought tears to the homeless man's eyes.

"Thank you very much. God bless you both," he said as he wiped his tears and watched Daniel and Isabella smile as they continued their walk to school.

CHAPTER 3: ATTITUDE

Rob and Andy were happy they were in the same class.

"Rob, hurry up. We are almost late," Andy called out to Rob.

They lived near each other and were happy they could walk to school together. Ms. Barbarisi, their teacher, was known to be a challenging teacher, but the students knew that she would take them on exciting field trips. She encouraged and inspired students to do their best. Since Rob wanted to be a lawyer, he knew that Ms. B would let him write a book report about being a lawyer.

As Rob and Andy walked into the classroom that morning, Eric was standing next to Ms. B with a big frown on his face. Ms. B had asked Eric if he would mind moving his seat where he had been placed alphabetically by his last name to make room for John, who was in a wheelchair and needed to be on the end of the row for easier access.

"But I won't be able to sit near my best friend," he complained to Ms. B.

When Rob and Andy heard Eric complaining, they pulled him aside and talked to him.

"He's in a wheelchair—he has to sit on the end of the row," Andy told Eric. "So wouldn't it be better if you had a good attitude about it rather than being grumpy?"

Rob chimed in and said that if Eric had a bad attitude, it would make John sad that he had to separate Eric from his best friend. Eric got the message. Why should he have a bad attitude? He should be more considerate. He quickly ran to Ms. B and apologized for not being cooperative at first. He explained that he had reacted that way because he would not be able to sit next to his best friend, but he realized that this was not the most important thing.

"I'm really sorry for that, Ms. B," Eric said politely. Ms. B was happy about Eric's change in attitude, and Andy and Rob were happy that it all worked out for the best. When John wheeled himself into the classroom minutes later, Ms. B explained that Eric had moved his seat so that John could have more space at his desk. John thanked Eric with a high-five, and Eric beamed with pride.

It was going to be a great year for everyone in Ms. Barbarisi's class!

CHAPTER 4: CIVILITY

Mai and Hannah had been best friends since kindergarten. They were both in the third grade at Lyncrest Elementary School. Their friendship was special because they both had a passion for science and math. Mai wanted to be a computer programmer and design virtual games she had seen on television science shows. And since Hannah wanted to be a physicist, they both read every book about science they could get their hands on, and they watched the movie *Apollo 13* seventeen times.

Both were excellent students and known for helping their classmates with the harder math problems. They spent every spare minute they had in the school library, where they read every book on space and astronauts and scientists. They were especially fond of the librarian, Ms. Scott, who found books she knew would excite their interests. Hannah's favorite astronaut was Susan Helms. Susan Helms served aboard the International Space Station and held the world record for the longest spacewalk of almost nine hours. They both hoped that they could work on space missions to Mars. Not only was Susan Helms an astronaut, but she was also a female general in the United States Air Force. Hannah and Mai thought that General Helms rocked.

One day as Hannah and Mai were in the library looking at the shelves lined with their favorite books, they heard their classmates Mary and Ella whispering to each other near the bookshelves.

"Ella, have you noticed something in class?" Mary started the conversation.

"Like what, Mary? There are a lot of things to notice in class," she replied, trying to find a book to read.

Mary giggled a little bit before she answered. "Did you notice that Isabella always wears the same clothes almost every day, and they are ugly and not in fashion?"

Hannah and Mai were shocked to hear Mary and Ella gossiping about their friend Isabella. They were both sad and mad at the same time. Isabella did not care for fashionable clothes, but her clothes were always clean and pressed.

Hannah and Mai walked over to Mary and Ella and told them that they had overhead their conversation. Hannah asked them to consider what would happen if Isabella found out they had been gossiping about her and to think about how hurt she would be.

"And I thought you both considered Isabella your friend," Mai said, explaining that if Isabella knew they were talking behind her back she would be angry and sad and very unhappy.

"How would you feel if someone was gossiping about you?" Hannah asked Ella and Mary. Hannah said that she would have been happy to hear them saying good things about Isabella when she was not around, but their saying mean things about her was gossip. "Saying things that would make someone unhappy when they are not around is not good manners," said Hannah.

Instead of taking part in the gossip, Hannah and Mai defended their friend Isabella. They tried to tell Ella and Mary that they were wrong to hurt Isabella. But when the girls continued on with their hurtful words, Hannah and Mai walked away to show that they were not happy with their behavior. The girls hoped they would realize their mistake one day.

CHAPTER 5: HONESTY

Andy and Mai's parents always taught them an important rule: "Do not lie." Their parents said that it would make their lives simpler. "You'll never have to remember what you told others. People will trust you as someone who always speaks the truth," Andy's father would say. They knew that even if it would get them in trouble, it was always best to tell the truth. Their parents said that when they were truthful their conscience would be clear.

One day Andy and Mai went to Mr. Martino's science class early. They loved to look at Mr. Martino's pet gerbil, Sam, that Mr. Martino kept in the class.

"He looks so cute. I wish he was mine," Andy said.

While watching Sam, Andy decided to open the lid of his container to get a better look at him. As soon as the lid came off, Sam scampered out of his container and out of the classroom.

Mai and Andy went running after him only to be met by Mr. Martino at the classroom door. They were both frightened and stood still in their tracks.

"Hi. How are you today? Are you both leaving already? I thought you loved staying in science class," Mr. Martino said.

Mai and Andy stood still, not knowing how to tell Mr. Martino that Sam was gone. But they knew that they always had to be truthful, even if the consequences would not be good for them.

"Y—yes, we do, sir, but …" there was a short silence as Andy stopped talking. They looked at each other, and finally Andy spoke up, "While we were trying to play with Sam, he escaped and ran out of the class. We are sorry, sir," Andy told Mr. Martino.

He had a very disappointed look on his face. He quickly alerted the school staff that Sam was on the loose so everyone would be on the alert to find him.

He then brought Mai and Andy into the classroom and sat them down.

"I'm very disappointed that you went against the stated rules that no one should open Sam's container," he told them. But he was pleased that they told him the truth about what had happened because now everyone would begin looking for Sam and hopefully find him. Mr. Martino said if they had not told him, he might not have known Sam was missing until the end of the day. Mai and Andy apologized to Mr. Martino.

Just as they were telling Mr. Martino how sorry they were for what they had done, Ms. Scott came into the classroom with Sam.

"I found him on top of a bookshelf after I heard the school announcement on the loudspeaker. Lucky for me, I was quick enough before he escaped again."

They were all happy. Mai and Andy volunteered to clean Sam's container for the next week to make it up to Mr. Martino. Mr. Martino said that their honesty was in part responsible for finding Sam because Ms. Scott had been on the lookout for him. So it worked out in the end, and Mai and Andy knew that honesty was always the best policy—just as their parents had taught them. They knew it was okay to make mistakes, but they should never lie about a mistake.

CHAPTER 6: KINDNESS

Isabella's and Rob's parents taught them to be kind. Isabella's mother told Isabella, "Kindness is not weakness."

Rob's father told him that it might be difficult to be kind when someone is being mean to you, but it is just when you are being treated unfairly and unjustly that your true character will show. "You shouldn't be mean back because you would be the same as the person being mean to you," Rob's father told Rob.

Isabella's mother said, "Always be kind and patient, because in the end those who treated you badly will be your best friends because of the kindness you show them."

Rob's mother said, "Think about people who have been kind to you. Do you not always remember their acts of kindness and think fondly of them? Do you not want to help them in their time of need?" She said, "We have to be kind to our neighbors and relatives and friends and even to those who are not kind to us because our kindness will show them the way to be."

Rob's mother said, "Have you ever wondered why you like certain people? The people you like and remember fondly are the ones who treated you kindly, the ones who went out of their way to help you. When you are harsh to someone, they will also remember you, but not fondly. They won't help you when you need help. They are the ones who may be happy if bad things happen to you."

One day while in the cafeteria eating lunch, Rob and Isabella noticed that Ella was sitting quietly by herself and crying. At a table in front of hers was her friend Mary. Mary and her friends were pointing at Ella and laughing at her. Ella was by herself, ashamed that she was being made fun of and sad that the girl she thought was her friend was now gossiping about her and treating her unkindly. Rob and Isabella walked over to Ella's table with their lunches and asked if they could sit next to Ella. Ella nodded with a smile and tears falling down her face.

"Why are you crying?" asked Isabella.

Ella said that when she would not let Mary copy her math homework, Mary became angry and told her that she was no longer her friend and was now making fun of her for being a goody-two-shoes.

Rob and Isabella told Ella not to worry because they would be her friends and to try to ignore Mary because she would hopefully soon realize that her behavior was bad.

Ella felt relieved and thanked Rob and Isabella. She also remembered how she had been gossiping about Isabella with Mary, and she felt very bad about that. Ella told Isabella what she had done in the library with Mary.

"I'm sorry for being mean, Isabella, and I will never gossip again. I promise!"

Isabella graciously accepted Ella's apology, and they all sat together, eating their lunch until the lunch bell went off. And they all walked happily to class. Isabella and Rob had a new friend, and Ella learned about kindness and why gossiping was bad. They knew that to be kind was the best way to be.

CHAPTER 7: GENTLENESS

Daniel and Hannah were waiting for the bookmobile to come to Lyncrest. Every Friday the bookmobile came so the students could choose up to five books to bring home for the weekend. Avid readers loved the bookmobile. It was Daniel and Hannah's favorite day of the week!

As they were standing in line, one of the students from another class, Megan, asked Daniel why his mother dressed funny. Megan said, "I saw you and your mother at the supermarket, and she had a thick scarf around her head in the heat of the summer. Why in the world does she dress that way? Doesn't she know it is summer? Your mother must have the seasons mixed up. She shouldn't be wearing a scarf all wrapped around her head in July."

Daniel's ears turned red. He thought Megan was mocking his mother because she wore a scarf for her religious beliefs. Hannah immediately saw Daniel's face and upset expression, and she pulled Daniel aside before he said or did something he would later regret.

"Daniel, I'm very sure Megan wasn't trying to be mean to you," said Hannah. "Megan has probably never seen anyone with a headscarf on their head except in the winter to keep themselves warm."

Hannah reminded Daniel that she had sometimes gotten upset when people made fun of her when she told them she could not eat pork. Hannah had to explain that she was Jewish and that she did not eat pork for religious reasons.

"Never say anything you will regret later. Try not to get angry, but try to understand the other person's point of view and that they are not making fun of you or your family. They might just be curious. That's what my father always tells me," Hannah told Daniel.

Hannah's father always told her to be slow to anger. "Getting angry will only make you do and say things that will upset you more later. People will then say that you have a bad temper."

Hannah's father told her about a famous businessman, Warren Buffett, who is one of the richest people in the world. Warren Buffett said that the best advice he ever got was his friend telling him, "Never forget, Warren, you can tell a guy to go fly a kite tomorrow. You don't give up that right. So just keep your mouth shut today and see if you feel the same way tomorrow." Hannah's father respected Mr. Buffett, who later said, "I don't know how many problems that saved me."

Daniel turned to Megan and said, "Megan, my mother wears a scarf for religious reasons, kind of like nuns who dress different."

Megan said, "Oh, that's neat. I didn't know that. That explains why she was covering up her head and ears in the summer."

And with that, they all happily climbed up the stairs and into the bookmobile, eager to choose their books.

CHAPTER 8: HUMILITY

Rob and Andy were in gym class, a favorite for most of the kids. They were playing dodgeball and hoping they would be one of the last ones to get out. Rob and Andy loved to play sports. Andy was a natural athlete and was very good at dodgeball.

Half of the class made a circle while the other half stood in the middle. Rob and Andy had the ball and were trying to get the other team out. Andy was great with his aim, and each time he threw the ball he hit someone out. When another boy, Tony, threw the ball, it went slowly, and the kids ran out of the way before the ball reached them. As Tony missed every shot, one of the kids on his team, Mark, began teasing Tony.

"Tony, why can't you make any shots?" Mark took the ball from Tony and said, "Just let me do it. You're going to miss it anyway." Mark made the shot and continued to hit the other team members, knocking them out of the game one by one.

All of the kids thought Mark was a show-off. They did not like how he hogged the ball and took it away from Tony. They liked Andy, who was just as good as Mark but wasn't a show-off. Even though Mark was good at all sports, he was never picked first by his classmates because he just showed off and put others down for not being as good as him.

Andy told Tony that he shouldn't mind Mark. Mark was just being arrogant, like his mother told him. She said that no one likes people who show off. "People will only like you if you are humble," she told him.

Andy's mom told him that arrogance was being rude and unkind to others who you think are not as good as you. She told him, "Even if you get the best grades and are the best in sports, do not brag to others. People like successful people who have good qualities or achievements but don't go around telling others about them."

She said that when she was in college, one of her classmates had a black belt in karate and had gotten into Harvard but decided not to go because he could not afford it. He also spoke four languages. But he never bragged about any of this. She found out by chance and respected him even more because he was not a show-off. She said this was the character of someone who achieved a lot but did not go around bragging about it to everyone. Andy's mom told him that he should never brag about how well he did on a test or his report card or anything else to make someone look bad. She said that people liked winners who were gracious and modest and humble.

When it came time to choose the gym sports captain, it was unanimous. Everyone voted for Andy. Mark got no votes. People like those who are not only good at the sport but who also help others and don't make fun of their teammates or hog the ball. Andy had good character; he was humble, not arrogant. That is why everyone voted for Andy to be their leader and gym sports captain.

CHAPTER 9: JUSTICE

Isabella and Mai were walking quickly to make sure they got to the front door of the library before anyone else. The library was doing spring-cleaning and clearing out their older books. The first people who arrived at the school library in the morning before the school bell rang would each get to pick two books to take home for free. Since Isabella and Mai loved to read, they asked their parents if they could get a ride to school extra early to make sure they had their first pick. When they got there, only one person, Fred, was in front of them. Fred loved to read too, so he must have made sure to be there before anyone else. Isabella and Mai were at least happy to have beaten the rest of the Lyncrest students.

"Good morning, Fred," said Isabella.

"Hi," said Mai.

"Good morning, Isabella and Mai," Fred replied as he smiled, eager to get his first choice of books. The librarian was not there yet, but they waited patiently.

Five minutes later, Fred waved at his friend, Richard, who was running down the hallway toward them.

Fred shouted out to him, "Come on, Richard, I've been saving a place for you." Richard eagerly slipped into the line right behind Fred and in front of Isabella and Mai.

Isabella and Mai turned to each other with scowls on their faces.

"That's not fair," said Isabella. "We came before Richard, and he shouldn't be able to cut in front of us."

Fred said they had made an agreement to save each other a place—whoever came first would save a place for the other one. Mai got very impatient and told Fred that was unjust.

"So, what if I saved a place for ten of my best friends, and they now got to cut in front of everyone else in line behind us—would that be fair? You have to be fair. It's not right that we came extra early and now someone who comes after us cuts in line in front of us. That's not how it's supposed to work. What's the point in making sure we came here first if others can cut in front of us?" said Mai.

Fred and Richard listened intently. Richard said, "You have a point. That wouldn't be just. I'll go to the end of the line. I wouldn't want someone who came after me to cut in front of me either. I just never thought about it that way." Fred agreed, and they were all satisfied.

Everyone wants to be treated fairly and justly. If you are treated unjustly, you feel angry and disappointed. Mai said her mother always told her to be fair. "Whether it is to a friend, relative, or someone you don't like, being fair is the right thing to do—whether you are rich, poor, popular, or unpopular," Mai's mother told her. She believed that people should be just and treat everyone as they would want to be treated. Being just means having your friend go to the back of the line if they came after others. Justice should be applied the same to everyone.

CHAPTER 10: PASSION

Rob's mother was a social worker, and she always told Rob that when he chose a career, he should be passionate about it. Passion, she said, was "loving your job so much that you would work for free."

Rob's mom loved helping low-income families and others who needed her services as a social worker. Work was not work for Rob's mother because she was so committed to her job that it was a calling for her. She could not think of doing anything else.

One day Rob and Andy were talking about what they would become when they grew up. Rob told Andy that his passion was to become a lawyer because when he saw the movie *To Kill a Mockingbird*, he admired the main character, Atticus Finch. He admired how Atticus fought for justice for those who had no money and who no one else wanted to help. Rob wanted to be just like Atticus and help people who were unjustly accused of crimes. He wanted to be a person who people could count on.

"My passion is to fly airplanes just as my father did in the United States Air Force," Andy said. "I want to protect those who are helpless and need protection from bullies. I want to keep America and the world safe by serving my country."

Andy and Rob shook hands and said they would both keep a pact to help people in their own way and always be friends. They promised each other that they would remind each other to go after their passion in life when they thought the other was going to settle for something that was not their passion but was just easy. The boys smiled as they finished their sandwiches and walked with excitement to their English class. They walked right to the dictionary and looked up the word *passion*. Rob read the definition out loud, "Passion: a feeling of unusual excitement, enthusiasm, or compelling emotion, a positive affinity or love toward a subject."

"Yes, that's what I feel when I think of becoming a pilot and astronaut," said Andy.

"Me too," said Rob. "When I think about a job where I will help people, I feel very excited."

They put the dictionary away and went to their seats, ready to learn as much as they could.

CHAPTER 11: POLITENESS

Daniel's mother always told him to be polite. "Be polite to the waiter at the diner, be polite to your teachers, and, of course, always be polite to your family, friends, and elders."

Daniel tried to listen to his mother's advice. Daniel was especially polite to his grandfather, who lived with his family. His grandfather had Alzheimer's and needed help from the family because his mind was not as sharp as it was when he was younger.

One day, Daniel brought Mai home with him after school to work on a group project. Daniel walked in the front door with Mai, and after they both took off their jackets, Daniel rushed to the family room to see his grandfather, who usually sat on the same couch in front of the television.

"Good afternoon, Grandpa," said Daniel with excitement.

Daniel's grandfather did not know what they were saying on TV, but he would sometimes walk up to the screen and try to talk to the people on the screen. He would sometimes get angry at the characters when they were speaking loudly. Daniel ran to his grandpa and gave him a big hug. His grandfather smiled, as he loved Daniel very much.

Mai gave Daniel's grandfather a big smile too. Daniel's grandfather looked at Mai with a blank stare, not knowing who she was. Mai walked to him and gave him a big hug just like Daniel did. Grandpa looked at her, wondering if she was his granddaughter. Mai had a big smile on her face, and Grandpa smiled back at her. Tears came rolling down his face as he saw the two young children who gave him such attention and kindness.

Daniel and Mai didn't know what Grandpa was thinking, but they were glad they were polite to him. They knew that he deserved to be treated with respect and kindness. As Daniel's mother told him, "Being polite means you should try to shake hands with a person and smile at them and be nice to people you meet."

Daniel's mom said that being polite meant smiling and having a cheerful face toward people. She had always told him that polite people did not look down on others; they tried to be helpful to others.

Daniel and Mai felt good about being polite and kind to Grandpa. They knew that their actions made Grandpa happy, and that was all that mattered.

CHAPTER 12: ACCOUNTABILITY

Hannah and Isabella had a project due for class the next day. While they had worked hard on it already, they still had a lot of work to do to finish it. They were sitting at Hannah's kitchen table with their papers, charts, and encyclopedias piled up.

Hannah was tired and felt nervous that they had so much more to do.

"I wish this wasn't due tomorrow!" she exclaimed to Isabella.

"What would happen if we didn't finish this and turned it in a day late? That way, we'd have time to get a better picture for the report."

Isabella's eyes widened. "Do you think it would be okay with Ms. Scott if we turned it in late?"

Before Hannah had a chance to answer, her mom, who was cooking dinner, turned to the girls. "Now, you know that if you have a homework assignment due you have to turn it in on time. That's the rule unless you have a good excuse, and I don't know what excuse you both have. Turning it in late just because you did not prepare well is not being accountable."

"Accountable, what does that mean?" asked Hannah.

Hannah's mother, who was also a teacher, said, "Well, if one of my students turned in a project late, there would be consequences. And the student would be held accountable. This means that you are responsible for your actions. If you don't do what you are supposed to do, you will be held responsible."

She said that unaccountable people have every excuse in the book. They tend to blame others, complain, put things off, and do the least amount of work necessary. She said that Benjamin Franklin, one of her favorite historic figures, said: "He that is good for making excuses is seldom good for anything else."

Hannah's mom said that if a project is due on a certain date, that's that. "You can't then make up your own rules along the way," she said.

Being accountable means you will deal with the consequences of your actions. Hannah's mom asked the girls, "What would happen if every student in the class just handed in homework whenever they wanted? That would not be good, and I don't think Ms. Scott would accept this either. Accountability is very important."

"Mom, okay, you're right," said Hannah.

Hannah enunciated the word slowly. "Accountability," she said. "Let's finish our project. We don't want to be unaccountable." They both worked hard for the next two and a half hours and finished their project. Hannah's mom prepared their dinner, which they ate quickly so they could have brownies for dessert. They ate the brownies and washed them down with a glass of milk. It felt good to finish their homework and even better to be accountable.

CHAPTER 13: BRAVERY

Andy and Isabella were sitting in class waiting for Mr. Martino to walk in. Behind Isabella sat the class bully, Marcus. Marcus started to kick Isabella's chair, and when she didn't turn around, he started to pull her pigtail, taunting her. "Hola, Isabella. Cómo estás, Mexicana?"

Andy's ears burned as he became angrier about Marcus teasing his friend.

Andy's father, a retired pilot who had flown fighter jets in the United States Air Force, always taught Andy to be brave and do the right thing. He told him to stick up for people who were not as strong as he was and help them when they needed help. Isabella did not retaliate, but Andy could not stand how Marcus was treating Isabella and looking down on her because her family was from Mexico.

Andy got up and stood right beside Marcus and told him to stop being a bully. "How would you like it if I taunted you? Do you think you are being brave by picking on people who choose not to fight back? Marcus, what if I started to pick on your sister and call her names, would you like that?"

Marcus said, "No."

Andy said, "Then don't do anything to others that you wouldn't want them to do to you or your family."

Marcus thought a minute and said, "Okay. I guess I never thought of it that way." He then sat down and said, "I'm sorry, Isabella."

Isabella smiled at Andy. She was happy to have a friend who was brave enough to stand up for her. She was lucky that Andy stood up for her.

Andy smiled back at Isabella. He was only doing what his father had taught him—to do the right thing.

CHAPTER 14: CHARITY

Rob's mom helped people at her job as a social worker. She also volunteered on weekends at a homeless shelter. She felt good when she could comfort people who were having a hard time in their life. So, when Rob's mom asked him if he wanted to help volunteer at the shelter on Saturday, he felt proud to be able to help. Rob asked if he could ask a friend from school to help too.

The next day, Rob asked Hannah, who jumped at the chance. She asked, "Will it be scary to be near homeless people?"

"No," said Rob. "My mom says that they are people just like you and me. My mom said they are people who are just having a hard time in their lives."

On Saturday morning his mom drove them to the shelter. She was happy they wanted to help. Rob's mom said that being charitable meant being merciful and helping others without judging them.

They got to the shelter in time to help serve food to the families who lived there. They served a hot breakfast that was donated by local restaurants. They helped put the eggs and toast on plates. They filled the cups with juice, tea, and coffee. Then they served the families who walked through the line. Hannah smiled as the families at the shelter thanked them for the breakfast.

Among the people were young children just like Rob and Hannah. After a long day, Rob and Hannah felt happy they could help people who had lost their jobs and homes.

Hannah told Rob, "I now know what it means to be charitable. It means to help others without judging them for being homeless. It means being kind and showing mercy to those who don't have the things we have."

When Rob's mom dropped Hannah off at her house, she said, "Thank you for letting me be charitable. I will never forget this day. Can I help out every month?"

Rob's mother smiled and said, "Sure, and maybe you can invite other friends from school next time, Rob."

Rob smiled. "Yes, let's invite a new person every week. Everyone deserves a chance to be charitable!"

CHAPTER 15: COMMITMENT

Mai promised her grandmother that she would help her on Saturday at the family's Chinese takeout restaurant. When Saturday came, Mai got up early, but she felt tired and wanted to go back to sleep and then go to Daniel's house to play later in the day because he had invited her to play.

Mai's mom did not look pleased. "Mai, did you tell Grandma that you would help her today?"

"Yes, but …" Mai said.

"Then you made a commitment, Mai, and she is relying upon you to help her today. Maybe one of her other employees won't be in due to an illness but she relied on you to keep your commitment. Because she relied on you to come in, she perhaps gave someone else the day off. If you don't go in, how will she be able to keep up with all the takeout orders? And when the orders are late, that will mean the customers will be unhappy, and they won't want to order from Grandma Li's shop anymore."

"Okay, Mom. I didn't think of it that way. I will keep my promise and commitment to help Grandma Li today," Mai said.

Mai's mom said, "That's my girl. I knew you would do the right thing, Mai."

"Well, I know I have to keep my commitment," Mai said, "because if I don't, I will cause Grandma Li to have a hard time in meeting the orders. That wouldn't be fair."

CHAPTER 16: COMPETENCE

"You have to develop competence in whatever you want to do in life," Isabella's mother said to her.

"What's competence?" Isabella asked.

Isabella's mom said, "It's being an expert at your job and being someone people come to for advice. When you know your job, people will look to you for answers."

"How do I become competent as a ten-year-old?" asked Isabella.

"Well, you study hard, especially the subjects you love and think you want to study in the future," Isabella's mom replied.

Andy, who was with Isabella, chimed in, "Yes, that's what my dad said. He used to fly jets in the United States Air Force. Dad said that his team trained when there was no war so that when there was a war, they would be competent to do what they were trained to do. They were successful because they trained hard before the real thing."

"So what this means to both of you is that you have to take school seriously and study hard because you never know what you'll need to be competent in for the future. You should study everything in school and do the best you can so that you can do your job properly when you need to get the job done!" Isabella's mom advised.

Isabella and Andy agreed that they would study hard so they could be competent.

CHAPTER 17: CONFIDENCE

Rob, his mom, and Hannah stopped by the local diner after their charity work on Saturday. Rob loved to eat brunch on weekends, and his mom liked to treat him on special occasions.

When the waitress came, Rob gave his order: "I want two eggs with toast and jam and hash browns with a large glass of orange juice, please." After they got their orders, Rob's mother noticed that Rob's toast was burned.

"Rob, why don't you ask the waitress to bring you new toast? Yours looks burned," she said.

"No, Mom, it's okay. I'll just scrape it off," he replied.

She looked at her son, knowing that he disliked burned toast. "Rob, it's not impolite to ask for what you paid for. When the waitress comes over, be confident but also polite, and tell her that your toast is burned and you would like new toast. You have to make sure you get what you ordered. The waitress is probably just busy and didn't notice that the toast was burned," Rob's mom said.

"Yes," said Hannah. "My mom always says that it is important to be confident. She said that it means being sure of oneself without being arrogant."

When the waitress returned, Rob looked up at her and said, "Ma'am, my toast is burned. May I have two new pieces of toast?"

The waitress looked at Rob and then looked at his toast. She seemed very sorry that his toast was burned. The waitress apologized to Rob, "I am so sorry, dear. Two new pieces of unburned toast coming right up for this nice young man."

She brought the toast to Rob right away, and with it she brought different types of jam and a side dish of blueberry pancakes with strawberries and whipped cream. She was so sorry, and she wanted to make it up to Rob.

Rob beamed with pride. "Thank you, ma'am. And thank you for the pancakes!"

When the waitress left, Rob's mom said, "See, Rob? If you are confident and polite, you will get what you asked for. No need to be shy and accept less than you ordered."

"That was a good lesson for me," said Hannah. "I used to think that asking for what you want is being pushy. But it's not."

Rob's mom agreed. She told them, "Being confident is just asking for what you deserve. It is not being arrogant. I am proud of you, Rob, and you were rewarded with delicious pancakes for speaking up!"

CHAPTER 18: COOPERATION

Mai, Daniel, Seth, and Laura had a group project to do for geography. They had to draw a map of the world, write about the continents, and find historical figures from each region of the world.

They sat down during lunch to decide how to work on the project. Daniel started, "How about we all pick one part of the world that we have an interest in and divide up the work? This way, we can each work on our favorite parts of the project and put together the best final project."

They all nodded their heads in approval.

"Now, that's cooperation," said Mai. "That's what my grandmother always says at the restaurant. If everyone does their job and works together, it all comes together, and the job gets done."

"Yeah, it means we all work together," said Seth. "We work together so it helps us all in the end."

"And when we all get to work on the parts we like—our passion—it's almost like we're not working because it will be fun," said Seth.

"Cooperation is cool," said Laura.

"Let's look up the word *cooperation*," said Mai. She found the word and read the definition from the dictionary: "The process of working together for a common purpose or benefit."

"Yeah," said Daniel. "The common purpose is getting our project done, and it benefits us all if we get our project done together." They all gave each other high-fives and smiled, ready to get the job done by cooperating.

CHAPTER 19: DUTY

Andy knew what the word *duty* meant. His dad always talked about "Duty, Honor, Country" from his United States Air Force days. So when Andy had a task to do, he would tell his friends, "It's my duty," and snap a sharp salute, just as he had seen his dad do many times.

Andy's father always said to him, "Never shirk your duty because people are counting on you." His dad was a hero and once rescued a fellow airman.

Mai also knew about duty, not from the military but from her grandmother's kitchen. When Mai was expected to pick up the bread rolls from the local bakery, she did her chores because it was her duty to do so and because people counted on her.

When Ms. Scott told the class she expected everyone to help the disabled student in class, Sidney, to make his day-to-day tasks easier, Andy knew exactly what he needed to do.

"I'll get the door," Andy yelled. Andy ran to the door to hold it open so Sidney could easily wheel his wheelchair through the door. And it wasn't just Andy who helped out; the whole class did. When Ms. Scott saw Sidney's classmates running to help Sidney take care of matters he could not handle on his own, she had a big smile on her face. Ms. Scott was the daughter of a military veteran, so she too understood the meaning of "Duty, Honor, Country."

Ms. Scott was very proud of her students. She smiled lovingly at them, happy that she had students with great character.

CHAPTER 20: DETERMINATION

Isabella knew what determination was. She watched her mother, a mechanical engineer, act with determination in everything she did. Her mom had immigrated to the United States from Mexico to go to college without knowing much English and with very little money. But she never gave up. She studied at night and worked during the day until she finished college, and in six years she got a job with a company helping to design airplanes.

Isabella's mom's determination to have a better life in America made her work hard until she achieved her goal. She never lost hope, even on the hardest days.

"Determination was what made the difference in helping me succeed," she would always tell Isabella.

This was the same determination that Isabella showed when trying to solve the difficult math problems that her teacher challenged the class with. Isabella never gave up. She never became frustrated because she knew that she would eventually understand the concept. Like mother, like daughter—determination to achieve her goals was what made the difference for Isabella's mom, and it was what Isabella knew would make the difference for her. It was determination that had made her get straight A's every year since the first grade.

When Mr. Martino called Isabella up to the blackboard to solve a problem, she would focus on the problem. With determination, she would solve the problem step by step, never giving up. Determination meant not getting frustrated but taking steps and working through the problem. Isabella was very determined, just like her mom!

CHAPTER 21: ENDURANCE

Daniel and Hannah both loved sports. Hannah loved to kick the soccer ball around her yard, and she would go to the park with her dad to practice her soccer skills.

Daniel had loved rugby ever since he saw the game played at the local college. "I would really love to play this sport," he said to himself. He knew he wanted to play rugby in college.

During gym class, Daniel and Hannah always ran the fastest and never stopped, even when they were tired. They never gave up because they knew that athletes needed endurance. Mr. Marks taught them the word *endurance*. He said, "Endurance is the strength to continue even when you are tired."

When Mr. Marks asked the kids to run around the track, Daniel and Hannah would run together to keep each other motivated. When Daniel got a little tired, Hannah would say, "We're almost done—let's keep going." And this would motivate them to continue.

"The more we run, the more we build up our endurance so that we will be strong when playing a game against other teams," Daniel would remind Hannah any time she got tired of running.

"That's right," Hannah said as they both made it around the track three times. "Yes! I endured!" shouted Hannah.

"And I am ready to beat our rival team next week because I don't think I will ever get tired. I am training with the best trainer in the world, Daniel!" exclaimed Hannah.

CHAPTER 22: EXCELLENCE

Mai and Rob were studying for their math test. They both loved math. Mai always tried to get a 100 on all of her math tests. She would study every day, even if she did not have a test coming up. Mai knew that it would take excellence for her to achieve her dream of becoming a computer programmer.

Rob studied hard too, but he did not like math. "I want to be a lawyer, so I don't think that math is important for me," he told Mai.

Mai said, "Rob, you should do the best you can at everything you try. My grandmother always says that I should aim for excellence in everything. She said that when you practice discipline and excellence in everything, it trains your mind to do well in everything you do."

Rob said," I guess you're right because if I want to be an excellent lawyer, I should train to be excellent at everything I do. Besides, who knows, math may come in handy in other things in my life, like going shopping and knowing how much money I have in my bank account."

Mai's grandmother always told Mai that she had to be excellent and try her hardest in everything. She said, "Mai, it doesn't matter if you are smart. The important thing is that you work hard. There are lots of children who are smart but do not try their best or care to improve. Mai, you need to be excellent in everything you do. Even when you sweep the floors of the restaurant, do your best to be sure it is as clean as possible. Put your heart into doing your best always. This is called excellence."

Rob gave Mai a high-five. "Yes, let us always try for excellence in everything we do," said Rob.

CHAPTER 23: FAIRNESS

Hannah and Rob were walking into their geography classroom. They both handed in their geography homework. Ms. Parsons had told the students that they had a week to complete the homework assignment and they could use any resource they wanted to. "There is only one rule: you cannot work with each other on this homework assignment," she instructed. They had to do the homework on their own.

As Rob was walking to his seat, he heard Mary Ellen telling Sandra that it was great that they got to use each other's books and work on the homework together.

"It took me less time to finish the homework assignment because I had a chance to work with you," Mary Ellen said.

Rob turned to Hannah, who also heard what Mary Ellen said. He was very surprised and said," Hannah, did you hear what I heard? We were not allowed to work together on this project. How is that fair that they worked together when Ms. Parsons said we shouldn't be sharing the work on this project?"

Hannah quickly turned to Mary Ellen and Sandra. "You know we weren't supposed to do a group project. You did not follow the rule that Ms. Parsons told us to follow. That is not fair. Why did you do that?"

Mary Ellen said, "Who cares? Ms. Parsons is not going to know."

"But that's not right," said Rob. "You knew that you could not do that."

Rob told Mary Ellen that his dad told him that you could tell a lot about people by how they act when no one is looking. This was exactly what Mary Ellen was doing, he thought. She was trying to break the rules, thinking no one was looking. Mary Ellen and Sandra looked at each other with guilt on their faces. They realized they had not done the right thing.

Mary Ellen and Sandra started walking to Ms. Parsons to tell her what they had done. This would only be the fair thing to do. If they told Ms. Parsons what they had done, she would at least know what to do to make sure it was fair for everyone else in the class who had followed the rules and had completed the homework on their own.

"Excuse me, Ms. Parsons," said Sandra. "We made a mistake and did not follow your homework instruction …"

Rob and Hannah were happy that Mary Ellen and Sandra did the right thing. Now it was up to Ms. Parsons to handle the matter. But at least Rob did the right thing to be sure that Mary Ellen and Sandra knew they were not being fair. Rob was happy that they had integrity and courage to tell Ms. Parsons the truth. Fairness was very important to Rob, and he was happy his friends did the right thing even when Ms. Parsons wasn't looking.

CHAPTER 24: FAITH

Before Daniel's grandfather got Alzheimer's, he used to tell Daniel to have faith. He used to say, "Daniel, do your best and then just have faith that things will work out for the best. But you have to do the work first. You can't just hope for things to be how you want. You have to take action to make it happen. Always remember that."

"What is faith?" Daniel asked his grandfather.

Grandpa had said, "It is a belief that things will work out for the best if we put our belief and trust in a higher power."

So when Daniel's grandfather started losing his memory and was diagnosed with Alzheimer's, Daniel never lost faith. "I'm going to stay strong and have faith that everything will be all right," he told himself.

Daniel decided that he was going to be a scientist and discover a cure for his grandfather to get better. He wanted his grandfather to get better, and he didn't want any other kid to lose his grandfather like he felt he was losing his own grandfather. He missed talking to his grandfather and telling jokes and stories. He missed his grandfather teaching him things like fishing and playing checkers with him.

Daniel had faith that his grandpa would one day have the medicine to be better, but he would not rely on faith alone. He would study hard and become a scientist to study the brain and the disease and find a cure for his beloved grandpa.

When Daniel went to bed each night, he prayed that he would be determined to study hard and become a doctor and a scientist to help his grandpa get better. He had faith that things would then work out for the best. Tears rolled down Daniel's cheeks as he thought of how much he loved his grandfather. He loved him so much, and he never gave up his faith that his grandfather would be better one day.

CHAPTER 25: FEARLESSNESS

Andy was known to be fearless in school. He was the one who confronted the bullies and spoke up to the teacher if the class did not understand the math problem or the homework. He was the one everyone could count on to do the right thing and not be afraid to tell a classmate that what he or she was doing was wrong or unkind. That's why everyone respected Andy. He had courage and was fearless.

One day, Andy and Mai were walking to school together. Mai told Andy that she was so lucky to have him as a friend.

Mai said, "Andy, I am very lucky to have such a good friend. Thank you for being my friend. I am glad that we met. What would we all do if you were not here to stand up to bullies and tell them what they were doing was wrong? You are always fearless."

Andy smiled at Mai. "You would do the same thing, Mai. You are also fearless and courageous. I am lucky that you are my friend too." Andy told Mai that his father told him that he had to have courage and not be afraid to speak up when someone was being hurt. Andy said, "Thank you for the compliment, Mai. I am proud to be courageous and fearless like my father. He was a pilot in the United States Air Force and always taught me to do the right thing and to stick up for people who are being bullied. I am glad that you think I am fearless like my dad."

Mai had a big smile on her face. "You're my hero, Andy, and I am sure the hero of lots of other kids at school!"

They both continued walking toward school for their first class of the day.

CHAPTER 26: FORGIVENESS

Isabella was known for never holding a grudge against others. When people did things to her that bothered her, she wanted them to know it was wrong and hoped they changed their ways.

Her mom always said, "If you think too much about these things, you will get the energy sucked right out of you. So just hope they come around and see your way."

One day as Isabella walked to the local ice cream shop, she saw Marcus asking for a chocolate ice cream cone. He loved the soft chocolate ice cream soaked with chocolate fudge. Chocolate was his favorite.

The girl at the counter asked him for the money for the ice cream cone. "That will be one dollar, young man."

Marcus dug through his pockets to find his coins. He had a disappointed look on his face when he told the girl that he didn't have enough money.

Isabella quickly grabbed fifty cents and ran over to Marcus and told him that she had extra change. Marcus looked down, embarrassed because he remembered how he had been mean to Isabella in class.

Isabella said, "Take it. It's okay—I have change I've saved up for the past three months. I have extra for you and extra for me too!"

Marcus looked up at Isabella and said, "Thank you, Isabella. I'm sorry I was so mean in school the other week. I was mean to you, but you are still nice to me." He had a sad look on his face.

"Oh, that's okay. You already apologized, so there's really no sense in thinking about what happened back then. It's over now," said Isabella. "Besides, I forgive you so long as you don't do that again to me or to anyone else."

"Oh, no. I never will," said Marcus.

They both smiled and began licking their soft ice cream as it dripped down the sides of the cones. They were all smiles now. Who wouldn't be?

CHAPTER 27: GENEROSITY

Rob's mom was known for her generosity. Every year she would go through the entire house and separate furniture, dishes, and clothes that they could afford to give away—things that were in good shape but that they didn't use that much. She asked Rob to also go through his room and choose clothes, toys, games, and books that he did not need. They would then go together as a family to the local homeless shelter and donate the items to the families who were going to rent an apartment, as they were now ready to move out on their own.

Rob always went through his stuff with excitement. He would look at a toy he liked but didn't play with much and realize he wanted someone else to enjoy it. He knew another little girl or boy would enjoy the item. His mom always said, "Sometimes you just want to keep everything, but just think how you would feel if you knew someone who couldn't afford your toy would enjoy playing with it and be so appreciative."

Rob knew she was right. He felt so lucky that he was not homeless and had a home to live in and never had to worry about sleeping in the cold or in a car. Rob was so happy to be helping.

"Mom, can I take a box to school so the other kids could bring in donations too?" he asked. "Then we would pick up the items from school and take them to the homeless shelter."

"Sounds like a plan," said his mom.

Rob was smiling from ear to ear. And he couldn't wait to tell the kids at school that they would be able to help the homeless children too.

"Thanks, Mom," said Rob. "I'll get all the kids at school to donate too. We're going to have lots of donations for the families. I can't wait. It feels good to help others."

CHAPTER 28: HOSPITALITY

Isabella's mom told her that she should always be hospitable. "What's hospitable?" asked Isabella.

"You have to make people feel at home when they visit you. When you go to someone else's house, how would you want to be treated?" said Isabella's mom. "You would want to feel welcome, wouldn't you? Wouldn't you be happy if your friend brought you treats and fruit punch and asked if you wanted to play a special game or have a favorite dessert? You want to treat your guest like she is a princess."

"That's great," said Isabella. "I want to make my friends feel special like princesses or princes when they visit me. I want to be hospitable just like you, Mom."

"Can we invite my friends to our house so I can make them all feel like princesses and princes?" she asked her mom.

"Sure," said Isabella's mother.

"And I'll make my special tacos and chili that Mai likes and the strawberry cheesecake that Hannah loves," Isabella said. "And I'll bake my special double chocolate chip cookies!"

Isabella was delighted because she was going to have a chance to be hospitable to her friends!

CHAPTER 29: HONOR

Andy's father told him time and time again about "Duty, Honor, Country."

"You never violate your honor and dignity. You never do anything that would disgrace you or your country," he told Andy.

"How do I become honorable?" asked Andy.

His father said, "Well, son, the best way to explain this is for me to read to you General Douglas MacArthur's speech to the cadets at West Point in 1962. General MacArthur said, 'Duty, Honor, and Country: Those three hallowed words reverently dictate what you ought to be, what you can be, what you will be. They are your rallying point: to build courage when courage seems to fail; to regain faith when there seems to be little cause for faith; to create hope when hope becomes forlorn … They make you strong enough to know when you are weak, and brave enough to face yourself when you are afraid. They teach you to be proud and unbending in honest failure, but humble and gentle in success …'

"This is what honor is, my son. It is never retreating when you fight. It is never being a coward. It is being willing to die for your country. For me, honor was when I was afraid, but I flew my plane to try to rescue my fellow airman because of duty, honor, and country."

"I am so proud that you are my father," Andy said as he gave his father a big hug. His dad pressed his head to his chest. Tears rolled down his cheeks as he remembered his friends who had died during their service together.

CHAPTER 30: INTEGRITY

Ms. Scott asked the class, "What is integrity?"

Hannah's hand shot up in the air, and Ms. Scott called on her to answer. "It's being honest and not lying," she said.

"Good, good," said Ms. Scott.

Rob chimed in, "It's being honest even when you're afraid of the consequences."

"That's right," said Ms. Scott.

Daniel put his hand up too. "My grandfather used to say that you should have integrity to do the right thing no matter what happens to you. He said that integrity meant you were truthful even if telling the truth made people dislike you for what you believed," he said.

"Integrity is being honest and trustworthy and doing what is right," said Hannah.

Hannah beamed with pride. She knew her friends trusted and liked her because she was always truthful. Hannah's mother had told her that when you have integrity you worry less because you don't say one thing to one person and another thing to someone else. She told Hannah, "Having integrity makes life easier. You can always be yourself. You don't have to change the way you are to different people. This makes you happier."

The students enjoyed the discussion about integrity in Ms. Scott's class. They all made a pact with Ms. Scott that they would always try to have integrity. Ms. Scott was very proud of her students. She was smiling; somehow she knew the children would act with integrity.

CHAPTER 31: LIBERTY

Mai was looking over her homework that was due to Ms. Scott that day. She felt proud of the time she had spent writing a paper about liberty. Liberty to her was freedom— freedom to do whatever you want to do, live where you want to live, be whatever you want to be, work where you want, marry whoever you want to marry, and be free. That was why her grandparents had come to America years ago. They wanted freedom.

Her grandmother said that she loved to live in a country where you could do what you want and achieve your dreams if you work hard. Mai's grandparents came to New York City, settled in Chinatown first, and started a noodle shop there before they moved out to the suburbs.

Mai's grandmother often said, "When there is liberty and freedom, you feel you can conquer the world and do whatever you want and have hope for yourself and your children. That's why we came to America, the land of the free and the land of the brave."

She said, "When we came here, the first thing we did was go and see the Statue of Liberty." "Lady Liberty" is what she liked to call it because the Statute of Liberty is a universal symbol of freedom in the world.

Mai wrote in her paper how the Statue of Liberty greeted millions of immigrants just like her grandparents, who were looking for hope and opportunity and a better life in America. She wrote that it was a symbol of freedom for people all over the world. This is why Mai was so excited to get to write about the meaning of liberty—because of what it meant to her family.

Mai was happy that her grandparents had come to America and that she had been born in America. She was grateful for her nice life and her fantastic friends. Mai's paper was titled: *America, Land of Liberty and Land of the Brave*. Mai was excited for Ms. Scott to read her paper because she worked very hard on it, and it had a special meaning to her. Mai was very grateful and happy for her life.

CHAPTER 32: LOYALTY

Daniel and Rob were waiting their turn to get to their gym lockers when they turned and saw Sam in line behind them.

"Hi, Sam," said Daniel. "Are you also waiting for your locker?"

"Yes," said Sam. "I've been waiting here too long and am getting a bit tired. Hey, by the way, did you hear that Isabella didn't come to school yesterday because she thought she was going to fail her math test?" Sam said. "That's what someone told me. She pretended to be sick so she could have an extra day to study. You know Isabella, she has to get a 100 on everything."

"Hey," said Daniel, "Isabella is our friend. You shouldn't be talking that way about her. That's not true, and it's not nice that you're making up stories about someone who isn't even here to defend herself."

"But it's true. She lied about being sick so she could stay home," said Sam.

Rob was getting upset. "Look, Sam, I went to Isabella's house after school and saw her yesterday, and the doctor was at her house checking on her. She has the measles. Didn't you know? She can't come to school for two weeks so she won't pass it to us. For you to go around spreading lies about her is not nice, Sam. That's not being a loyal friend. And, besides, it is not true—it is a lie."

Rob said, "My mom always says that it's important to be loyal to your friends and support them. She said that we would want them to do the same for us if we were being talked about or attacked when we were not there to defend ourselves."

Sam looked embarrassed. "Well, I was told that she was faking it."

"Yeah," said Daniel, "that's what you thought, and without knowing it, you were spreading these lies about her. I hope you learned your lesson."

Sam said he was sorry. "I'll go visit Isabella when she is not contagious anymore and apologize to her myself."

"That sounds like a good idea," said Rob. "We'll all go together and show support for our friend. And we'll take Isabella her favorite ice cream too!"

"Yes, let's do that," said Sam. "It's the least I can do to make it up to her."

CHAPTER 33: MERCY

Rob always said he wanted to be a lawyer because he wanted to fight for justice. "I want to make sure that people are treated fairly. And when I go to court to defend them, I am going to make sure I protect their rights."

"That's great," said Hannah. "I know you will be a great lawyer because you have mercy. My mom said that showing mercy to people is important because sometimes they make mistakes and can be forgiven."

Rob said, "Yes, I hope that the judge shows mercy for my future clients when I go to court because I may not always win."

Hannah said, "My mom also told me that sometimes people have the power to punish you, but they can show mercy too and treat you kindly if you regret what you did. I guess showing mercy is like being compassionate and kind."

"Yes, it's like when we go to the homeless shelter and help the families who are having a hard time in life," Hannah added. "We are showing them mercy and kindness to help them when they are in a desperate situation."

"Yes, that's what I am going to do when I'm a lawyer—show mercy to my clients. And I hope when I need mercy, someone will be merciful to me too," Rob said, smiling.

"Me too," said Hannah. "I hope people will have mercy for me too."

They high-fived each other and smiled. They knew that it was important to have mercy and help others. They knew they would always help each other out because they were friends.

CHAPTER 34: MODESTY

Ms. Scott was handing back the homework assignments to the class. She patted Isabella on the head and said, "Perfect. Isabella, I loved reading your essay."

Isabella looked down, embarrassed that Ms. Scott complimented her loud enough for the rest of the class to hear. When she looked up, all eyes were on her. Isabella did not like to show off when she did well. She did not want the other kids to know her grades. Isabella's mom had told her that it was better to be modest.

She told Isabella that being modest didn't mean that you shouldn't be confident. "Being modest just means that you don't brag about how well you've done. Others may resent you and be jealous if you do. But when you are so good at many things and don't show off, people will admire you and respect you," her mother told her.

Isabella looked back at Ms. Scott and smiled. "Thank you," she said.

Isabella's mom had said, "While you should not be a show-off, this doesn't mean that you shouldn't be gracious and thank people when they compliment you." This is why Isabella thanked Ms. Scott.

Rob smiled at Isabella and said, "You worked hard on that essay, Isabella. Great job! You deserve the good grade you got."

Isabella and Rob knew that working hard is always what makes you successful. You didn't succeed by getting lucky but by working hard and studying hard. They both also knew that they liked their friends who were modest and not show-offs. Isabella was modest, and so was Rob. That's why they got along so well. They were modest just the way their parents taught them to be.

CHAPTER 35: MOTIVATION

Hannah and Rob were known as good athletes among the kids at school. Hannah could be seen kicking her soccer ball in the air, and Rob loved to clutch his rugby ball that all the kids thought was a funny-looking football.

One day Hannah asked Rob, "Hey, Rob, do you want to run a 5K with me and my mom? It's for a good cause—to raise money for Alzheimer's research."

Rob asked," What's 5K?"

"Let's do the math," said Hannah. "It is a race that is 5 kilometers long." She took out the calculator and figured out that 5K was about 3.1 miles.

"Wow, that's a long race, but we can do it," said Rob.

"Yeah, piece of cake," said Hannah.

"I'm in," said Rob.

"This will be fun. How about we ask the other kids to run with us too?" Hannah suggested.

"That's a great idea, Hannah. Then we'll even raise more money. And running with our friends will make us more motivated to finish the race," said Rob.

Hannah said, "Let's meet after class with the others and come up with a schedule to make sure everyone is ready and can finish the race. We have a month to prepare. I am sure we can do it."

After the school day was over, the group all met in the school cafeteria. The group was Mai, Daniel, Hannah, Rob, Isabella, and Andy. They talked about the race and came up with a schedule of how many miles they would have to run each week to make sure they would be able to run a total of 5K on the day of the race. Their eyes lit up as they became very excited and motivated to run together. They knew that they would be able to accomplish their goal if they trained together and kept each other motivated.

The best part was that they were excited to be helping a good cause—Alzheimer's research, which was important for their friend Daniel. This made them even more motivated. They couldn't wait to begin training!

CHAPTER 36: OPTIMISM

Andy was always smiling. Sometimes kids at school would ask him why he was always smiling. Andy said, "I'm happy because I have a lot to look forward to in life. I can't wait until I can hopefully go to the United States Air Force Academy and become an Air Force pilot like my father and an aeronautical engineer and then an astronaut!"

Andy said that his dad always told him, "There are two types of people in the world. There are those who look at the glass as half full and those who look at the glass as half empty."

Daniel laughed, "I'm a half-full person!"

"Yes, you are," said Andy. "That means we're both optimistic. That's what Dad says, 'The glass-half-full people always look at the good side of things.'"

"So, the half-empty-glass people must be pessimists," said Rob.

"I guess so, but we're not pessimists. No reason to be." They all high-fived each other and finished their lunch.

"Optimists. I kind of like the sound of that," said Mai. "I'm an optimist too!"

CHAPTER 37: PATIENCE

Hannah liked to get things done. She would have an idea and want to get it done right away. While Hannah was excited about running a 5K, she told her mom, "I want to run a marathon next—a real-life marathon."

"A marathon?" asked her mom. "You mean twenty-six miles?"

"Yes, I want to run that in two months," Hannah said.

"Whoa, whoa," said Hannah's mom. "The way you achieve a goal is step by step. Yes, you want to achieve the goal, and that's great. But you have to have a plan and work hard one step at a time. You have to have patience so you can go through the steps to achieve the goal you want. You can't just rush into it without thinking or making a plan to know how long it will take you to be ready to run that many miles. You have to start out slow. First run the 5K, and then we can consider the other races. It takes hard work and time to gain endurance so you can run longer distances. This doesn't happen overnight," Hannah's mom told her.

Hannah's mom noticed that her daughter was looking sad. She walked toward her and said, "Hannah, I find it admirable that you want to run a marathon, but let's work up to it. Let's first do the 5K, then a 10K, then a half marathon, which is 13 miles. And when you are old enough to run a marathon—you have to be at least fourteen years old—you'll have the training and skills to be a full marathoner!"

Hannah said, "Okay. Then patience means that you have to take the steps to be ready for the big run and not expect to achieve it right away."

"That's right," said Hannah's mom. "It's like learning to be a world champion tennis player. Do you think Serena Williams became a tennis champion overnight? No, she worked hard, starting when she was three years old. And step by step, she worked and trained to become the best tennis player. It takes patience and hard work, one step at a time, to achieve any goal you want in life. Consistent action and patience," she said.

"I am going to be patient and also work hard to prepare to run a marathon one day, Mom. Because if I am patient, I will do anything I set my mind to." She gave her mom a high-five and skipped toward the back door to go talk to Rob about her big plans.

CHAPTER 38: PERSEVERANCE

Mai's grandmother had worked hard since she immigrated to the United States. She started by opening a tiny noodle shop, where she had enough money to cook small bowls of noodles and put her special spices and sauces into the soup. Although Mai's grandma's shop was tiny, people still lined up to buy the soup because it was so tasty. There was no noodle shop anywhere that had the soup her grandma made. Through hard work, the family grew the tiny soup shop into a larger shop. After ten years it became a very popular takeout restaurant, and it was also popular for workers during lunch.

While Mai's grandmother's soup restaurant was popular around the town, it did not happen overnight. Grandma Li worked day and night to grow the business. She once had to shut the soup shop down when she had pneumonia because no one else could cook her special soups. She almost lost the shop, as they couldn't keep up with the rent payments. These were tough times for Mai's grandma. But she never gave up because she had perseverance.

At times they had no money to buy new clothes and could not afford to buy meat, but they never gave up. When Mai's grandmother, Li, got better after her illness, she started teaching others how to make the soups so that if she got sick, someone else could take over. It took a lot of perseverance, but things got better, and now they were doing very well and had opened up other restaurants in surrounding towns.

Mai's grandmother always told Mai that success did not come overnight. "It took time and failing, but we never gave up. I always got back up and never felt sorry for myself. Feeling sorry for yourself won't do you any good," she told Mai.

Mai's grandmother was so appreciative for her good fortune that she often gave food to the homeless people who came into the shop to escape the cold. She let them sit in the corner and asked the restaurant workers to give them hot soup.

She said, "You never know when you will also be in their position. Best to help those you can, Mai."

Mai asked her grandma if perseverance meant never giving up. "Exactly," she said. "It means you keep trying. Because it's right when you want to give up when you will succeed."

Mai gave her grandma a big hug. "Thank you for being a good example of perseverance for me, Grandma. I love you!"

CHAPTER 39: PERSISTENCE

Isabella was sitting with Hannah, talking about how they would one day be in high school.

"I hope you never move away from Lyncrest," said Isabella.

"Oh, I won't move. This is my town. I don't ever want to leave my friends," said Hannah.

"Let's keep a promise that we always stay together. Let's promise that we'll never move away, and that we'll graduate from high school together at Radburn."

"That's a plan," said Isabella.

"And maybe we'll go to the same college one day," said Hannah.

"I hope so," Isabella replied. "Not like my mom, who had to leave her own country and come to the United States for a better opportunity in life. My mom said that she had to be very persistent to reach her dream. She came to the United States alone and knew no one. She didn't have a lot of money, but she had hopes and dreams to be an engineer. My mom told me that she never gave up, even when it was very tough. Mom told me she had to go to school at night while she worked during the day. She would be very tired at school and would sometimes feel like falling asleep. But she said that she drank coffee to keep her awake to study."

"Wow, your mom was very brave and strong," said Hannah. "Isn't it great that she came to the United States, and you were then born in America?"

"Yes," said Isabella. "Now I have lots of opportunities and can go to college here, and hopefully I can go during the day and not have to work during the day like my mom did. But I'll do what I have to do. I know that I will have persistence like my mother. I will never give up until I reach my goal," Isabella said with determination.

"That's cool," said Hannah. "My mom told me that I should be persistent too. She said, 'Hannah, you have to be persistent if you want to run a marathon or do anything in life. Just keep going, and never give up.'"

"I'm so glad that your mom came to the United States," said Hannah. "If you hadn't come here, I would never have met you."

"Yes, and now we're the best of friends. Okay, let's make a pact to stay in the same school and also to be persistent together and never give up!" They smiled and high-fived each other.

CHAPTER 40: PRINCIPLE

Andy's father told him that you have to be principled in everything you do.

"What's principled?" asked Andy.

"Andy, have you heard the phrase, 'If you're going to talk the talk, you have to walk the walk'? What this means is, if you're going to tell someone to do something, you should also do the same thing. Andy, this means that if I told you that you shouldn't smoke because it is harmful for you, then I shouldn't be smoking either, as you will be asking me why I am smoking if I am giving you advice not to smoke. This would not make sense, would it, Andy?"

Andy's father said, "Being principled means standing up for your beliefs and not saying things that you think will impress others even if you don't believe what you're saying. Being principled means doing what you think is right even if others will not like what you are saying because they don't agree with you,".

"It is staying true to your character, your values, and your beliefs, and not changing your beliefs because you want others to like you. That's being principled. If you are principled, people may not agree with you, but they will respect you, Andy," his father told him.

Andy's eyes widened, and he smiled at his father. "Dad, I've never heard you tell me to do something that you don't do yourself. I've never heard you tell me to not do something that you do. So I know you are principled, and I want to be just like you. I want to walk the walk just like you!"

Andy's dad smiled and gave Andy a sharp salute. "You will make one good United States Air Force officer and leader one day, Andy. I am so proud of you!"

Andy hugged his father as he thought how lucky he was to have a principled father.

CHAPTER 41: RELIABILITY

Daniel loved to take his grandpa for walks when he came home from school.

"I like taking my grandpa for walks because he's inside the house most of the day. I like to take walks with him so he can exercise and enjoy the fresh air," Daniel told Hannah.

Grandpa could always rely on Daniel for their daily walks. Rain or shine, Daniel was always reliable because he didn't want to disappoint his grandpa.

Daniel loved the way his grandpa would smile when he saw Daniel coming through the door and running toward him as he dropped his book bag on the kitchen table. Daniel would get his grandpa's shoes and coat on and take him by the arm to the front door. Daniel would walk on the sidewalk of their street, down to the end of the street and back. Gramps would smile at Daniel as he shuffled along the street, gripping Daniel's hand real tight so he wouldn't let go.

Daniel's mom smiled when she saw her son being so attentive. She loved how her son was so caring and compassionate toward his grandpa. She leaned over toward Daniel's dad and said, "He is always so reliable. It's so nice that Gramps can always rely on Daniel. What a good boy he is. I am so proud of Daniel,".

CHAPTER 42: RESPONSIBILITY

Isabella had lots of homework due the next day. She was thinking about what she would tackle first when she got home. As she sat looking at her homework planner, Sally came by and said, "Hey, Isabella, let's get ice cream at the ice cream shop. They have free sprinkles today."

Isabella's eyes lit up—she loved the chocolate and rainbow sprinkles at Eddie's ice cream shop even more than the ice cream itself.

"Sally, I'd love to, but I have to get home and finish my homework. I also promised to help my mom with an errand today," Isabella said.

"But you're missing out," said Sally. "Your mom will understand when it comes to ice cream. She can do the errand herself."

"But I promised her," said Isabella. "I know she's counting on me. Mom always says that if you make a promise, you need to keep it. It shows that you are responsible. And, besides, I have homework for tomorrow. I need to make sure Ms. Scott knows I am responsible too."

"Have it your way," said Sally. "All the kids will be there. You're just missing out."

"Thank you," said Isabella. "I hope I can go with you another time." Isabella knew that she was doing the right thing.

Sally walked away feeling upset that Isabella would not go with her to get ice cream. But Isabella was just being responsible. That was always what her mom taught her to be. She always said, "Isabella, it is very important to be responsible. Make sure people can trust you and rely on you, and keep your word to them."

Isabella knew that being responsible was more important than ice cream cones any day! Besides, her mother was counting on her; she would not let her down.

CHAPTER 43: RESPECT

Daniel was lying on the couch, watching his favorite anime cartoon on TV. His legs were sprawled across the couch. Daniel's grandfather walked into the family room.

"Grandpa!" Daniel jumped to his feet to help his grandpa put on his slippers.

He gave his grandpa a big hug and held him very tight. He loved his grandpa and respected him very much. He knew that to respect his grandpa meant to honor him. After all, his grandpa had worked very hard when he was a younger man and had helped his children and grandchildren in every way he could.

Daniel's mom said it was important to respect your elders. "You should honor them and get up if you are sitting down when someone older comes into the room. It's just acknowledging the person and making sure they know that you care about them." Daniel's mom said it wasn't good manners to be lying down when an older person walked into the room. "Stand up as a sign of respect for them," she told him.

She said that Daniel should show everyone respect. "Treat others like you want to be treated," she told Daniel. She also reminded him to be respectful to all of his teachers, his relatives, and his friends.

"When you respect someone," said Daniel's mom, "you will treat them well." Daniel never forgot what she taught him. And Daniel was never disrespectful to anyone, especially his most dear grandpa. He smiled as he squeezed his grandpa's hand really tight. He was happy to have his grandpa and to be able to show him respect.

CHAPTER 44: SHARING

Each year Hannah's mom would cook three extra turkeys during Thanksgiving and distribute them to the homeless shelters. She knew the shelters had more residents during the colder months, and she wanted to be sure the families had special meals during the holidays.

Hannah was telling Rob about the turkeys her mom would cook when Andy said, "Why don't we all help your mom cook special food and desserts so we can help the homeless shelter take care of the families this Thanksgiving?"

"That's a great idea," said Hannah. "I'll send a message to everyone so we can all meet after school and plan what we want our moms to cook."

They all met at the cafeteria after school and made a list of the turkeys and stuffing, pies, and cookies they would help to prepare for the shelter.

"This turned out great," said Andy. "And that's why they call it Thanksgiving. It's to share and help our community and to give thanks for all that we have. We are lucky that we have great friends and family."

"Sharing is caring!" said Mai. "My grandma says that when you share food, your food tastes even better."

"I can't wait to start to help my mom and dad with all the cooking," said Andy.

"I love to bake chocolate chip cookies," said Isabella.

"This is going to be the best Thanksgiving ever!" they all shouted.

CHAPTER 45: SELFLESSNESS

While Andy sat in the cafeteria at lunch, he was trying to remember the math word problems that might be on the test next period. Since the beginning of the school year, he had worked hard to try to solve all types of math problems to become an expert. He wanted to be a pilot and aeronautical engineer, so he thought that math might be pretty important.

Seth came and sat near Andy and asked, "Andy, I am having trouble solving this problem. I am just stuck. Can you help?"

"Sure," said Andy. "Let's see. Oh yeah, you just have to take into consideration that Sue's mom drove the car at sixty miles per hour. You need to consider that the trip took five hours and factor that into the equation. So here's how you would go about solving the problem."

"Wow, you made this seem so easy, Andy. You're so good at math," Seth said.

"Well, it just takes practice, actually. I'm no better than you, but I practice and study these problems a lot so that it becomes easy after awhile. Do you need help with any other problem, Seth?" asked Andy.

"But you have to finish studying for the test, don't you?" Seth asked.

"No, that's okay. I have time to help a friend," Andy replied.

"Okay, how about this problem? I'm stuck on this too," said Seth.

Andy showed Seth how to figure out the problem with an easy step-by-step approach. Seth was amazed. For some reason, it all just seemed to click.

Hannah was sitting next to Andy and Seth, listening to Andy carefully as he helped Seth get ready for the math test.

Hannah said, "Andy, you are selfless. That's a new word I learned in history. It means helping others even before yourself—putting others first. You could have been studying and getting ready for the test yourself, but instead you are helping a friend before yourself."

"You are kind, Hannah. But I'm not selfless. It's my dad who is selfless."

Andy's dad did not care if there was danger and he would possibly die. He only cared about his fellow airmen and trying to rescue them, even if it meant he would die trying. Explaining this to his friends, Andy said, "That is what it means to be selfless! And if I am a little like my dad, then I am very happy. Thanks for the compliment, Hannah,".

Seth turned to Andy. "Well, I think you are selfless just like your dad. And I think I am going to get a 100 on this test because of you!"

CHAPTER 46: SELF-CONTROL

Daniel and Mai were sitting on the bench in front of their school. Sam was at the tetherball court, swinging the ball around really fast. As he was playing, Jeffrey walked toward Sam.

"Hi, Sam," said Jeffrey as he waved.

Sam said, "Come on over. Let's play a game of tetherball." As Jeffrey walked toward Sam, Sam swung the ball as hard as he could toward Jeffrey's head. It hit Jeffrey smack on his head.

Jeffrey screamed out, "That hurt. What was that for?"

Daniel and Mai saw what had happened, and Daniel went running toward Jeffrey to see if he was all right. Daniel's ears were red because he was so upset with Sam. Mai ran with Daniel toward Jeffrey. Mai said, "Let's help Jeffrey first, and then we can talk to Sam after we are sure Jeffrey is okay. And let's not do or say anything to Sam that we will regret later," she told Daniel. Mai knew that Daniel was very upset with Sam, and she wanted to be sure they did the right thing.

Mai said that her grandmother always told her that a very important thing in life is to be able to control your anger. You don't want to do something that you will regret later.

"Sam was very mean to Jeffrey. We need to teach him a lesson on why what he did was very bad," Daniel said to Mai.

Daniel looked at Jeffrey's face and noticed that he did not have any bruises or blood; he asked him if he was okay. Jeffrey said, "Yes. It hurt really bad at first, but I am okay now. Thank you, Daniel."

Daniel and Mai then approached Sam and asked how he would like it if they started throwing balls at his head really fast.

Sam's eyes widened. "Oh, no, you wouldn't?"

"Well, why are you doing that to Jeffrey, then? You hurt Jeffrey. Don't you feel bad?" Mai asked.

"Yeah, but Jeffrey doesn't mind."

"What?" shouted Jeffrey. "What do you mean I don't mind? That hurt my head a lot. And you could have broken my glasses."

Sam thought for a minute. "Aw, Jeffrey, I didn't mean it. I guess that was a stupid prank. I'm sorry. Are you okay, Jeffrey?"

"I think I'm okay, but I hope you never do this to anyone again," Jeffrey said.

"I won't," said Sam. "I'm sorry, Jeffrey."

"Thank you, Mai," said Daniel. "I would have made things worse if I had done or said something that I would have regretted later," said Daniel. "I just hope that Sam learned a lesson about self-control and realized what it would feel like if he were in Jeffrey's shoes." Daniel said, "Having self-control made it turn out a lot better. Otherwise, we'd all be at the principal's office right now. Self-control is important so we don't do stupid things when we are mad."

Mai agreed. She said, "Sam had no self-control, but I hope he learned a lesson."

CHAPTER 47: SINCERITY

Mai and Isabella were sitting in the cafeteria, eating their sandwiches. They both loved peanut butter and jelly, and they had the same sandwich almost every day. Isabella's mom told her that she should add some variety, but Isabella loved peanut butter and insisted that she have it every day. Her mom did make different sandwiches to add some variety and surprise Isabella, but she still wished she had a peanut butter sandwich for her lunch every day.

The girls looked into their lunch boxes to see what snacks their moms had surprised them with. Isabella had popcorn and sliced oranges and Mai had almonds and raisins.

Shirley, their friend, was sitting all alone at the end of the table. Mai and Isabella noticed that she wasn't eating lunch and looked sad.

Mai went over to ask Shirley why she wasn't eating.

"I forgot my lunch today," she said.

"Oh my, let's get Ms. Johnson to get you a school lunch from the cafeteria line today, Shirley."

"No, I am too embarrassed," said Shirley.

"That's not something to be ashamed of. I forgot my lunch many times. But if you don't want to get lunch from school today, you can share my sandwich and snacks. Isabella and I have plenty to share," said Mai.

"Yeah," said Isabella. "Peanut butter and jelly sandwiches. That's what we both have today."

Shirley's eyes lit up. "That's my favorite!"

"Well, then, come on over."

Mai and Isabella gave Shirley half of their sandwiches and some of their snacks. Now Shirley had a whole sandwich. She started eating the sandwich, and a smile came across her face. "Thank you, Mai and Isabella."

"We're happy you like your lunch," Mai said with sincerity.

"That's what friends are for. Friends help and look out for each other," Isabella said.

Isabella said that her mom told her, "If you are sincere and care about your friends, they will care about you too. Being sincere means to really care and show that you care through your actions."

"I am sure your mom would be proud of both of you today," said Shirley. "And, I will always remember your sincerity."

CHAPTER 48: TEAMWORK

Andy, Hannah, and Rob were sitting at the baseball field behind the school, talking about what they were going to do over the weekend. One of the school custodians, Mr. Paul, was emptying the trash cans at the field. The bins were full of plastic water bottles, juice boxes, and candy wrappers from the baseball game over the weekend. Leagues used their fields to play games, and the trash bins were full. As Mr. Paul lifted the trash bin to empty the contents into his large black plastic trash bags, the garbage went flying all over as a gust of wind scattered the trash. Mr. Paul looked frustrated at the water bottles now lying on the ground.

"Hey, let's go help Mr. Paul," said Andy.

"Yeah," said Hannah. "With us all helping him, we'll be able to clean up the mess in no time."

"Yes," said Rob. "That is called teamwork. We can get a lot more done if we all work together."

They all helped Mr. Paul pick up the trash, and the trash was all picked up and placed in the plastic trash bag quickly.

"Thank you, kids," said Mr. Paul with a smile on his face. "You just saved me a lot of work. Now that's teamwork. I could not have gotten this done without you! Thank you for being on my team," said Mr. Paul.

Andy, Hannah, and Rob smiled at Mr. Paul, happy that they could help him. They knew that teamwork made everyone's job easier.

CHAPTER 49: TENACITY

Rob was sitting at the kitchen table, doing his homework while his mom was cooking dinner. The TV was on in the family room, and he heard the newsman say, "It took a lot of tenacity for Thomas to achieve his dream under the most difficult circumstances, but he did it. Thomas Sanders spent a good part of his high school years living with his family in a homeless shelter after his father lost his job and his mother passed away…"

Rob's ears perked up as he listened to the story of Thomas Sanders, who through all the problems and difficulties of living in a homeless shelter, was still able to study hard, persevere, and not give up until he realized his dreams of going to college.

Thomas studied so hard that he was able to get a scholarship to Harvard. Despite his family's poverty, he studied day and night and got straight A's throughout his four years of high school. All of the teachers at school wrote glowing remarks about Thomas, especially about how he never gave up and had tenacity despite his family's situation.

"Wow, that sure is tenacity," said Rob. "I am never giving up until I become the best lawyer in America one day."

"Well, if you have tenacity and work hard like Thomas, you can. Tenacity just means that you never give up until you reach your dream—*never*," said Rob's mom.

"I like that," said Rob. "I want to be a tenacity person just like Thomas Sanders."

"You will be a *tenacious* person," she said, correcting Rob. "You too are tenacious and will achieve great things with hard work. I am so very proud of you, Rob."

Rob smiled and hugged his mom. "Thanks for being my mom!"

CHAPTER 50: TOLERANCE

Daniel and Hannah were in history class while Mr. McDaniel was explaining historical cases of intolerance. He talked about the Holocaust and how Hitler's intolerance and hatred for the Jewish people caused the extermination of six million Jewish people and millions of others in death camps. He explained that being tolerant of other religions, races, cultures, and nationalities was part of what it meant to live in America.

"Just think of it this way. Everyone is born a certain way by chance. You are either born black or white or brown or any other color. The color of your skin does not matter, it is your character that counts," he said.

Tolerance means you may believe in another religion or no religion, but you should never tell someone else that your religion is better than his or hers or that they have to believe what you believe. It is tolerance that made America so great! It's because we are people from all over the world.

Hannah's hand went up. "My grandparents came from Eastern Europe and escaped from Hitler."

"And my family came to America for freedom," said Daniel. "My mom says that she feels freer to practice her religion and dress the way she wants in America than anywhere else in the world."

"America is tolerant," said Mr. McDaniel. "Which is why talented and bright people from all over the world come here to use their talents to their full potential. And I am glad your ancestors came to America, as I have gotten to know you because of that."

They were all beaming with pride and happy they lived in America, home of the free and home of the brave.

CHAPTER 51: TRUSTWORTHINESS

Rob said that his mom told him that one of the most important things is being trustworthy.

"Why?" asked Isabella.

Rob replied, "She said, 'If people don't trust you, then you'll never be able to have a good relationship with them. 'Mom said that she once had a friend who lied to her about needing money. She told my mom she needed it to repair their home's heater. It turned out that she used the money to buy herself expensive jewelry."

"Wow. How can she lie like that?"

"That's the point," said Rob. "My mom will never be able to trust her again. How could she? Once you lie, it's hard for anyone to trust you or take you seriously. Which is why I guess when I didn't get my homework done for math, I told Mr. Martino the truth. I told him that I did not get the homework done. I did not lie and say that I forgot the homework at home."

"You are trustworthy all right, Rob," said Isabella. "I'm sure glad that you are my friend."

"You are trustworthy too, Isabella. That's why you are my friend!"

CHAPTER 52: WISDOM

"You will gain wisdom one day," said Mai's grandmother.

"Why can't I have it now?" asked Mai as she helped her grandma clean the counters at the soup shop.

"You are very smart, Mai. But wisdom is something you acquire with time. You gain it with experience, with time and knowledge. You know how to make better decisions and have better judgment. That's why in important matters we say that you should ask your elders for advice. Because older people have lived through the things you are experiencing and can offer you advice on such matters. That's why your mom and I like to talk to you about our experiences and mistakes. Because we've made a lot of them, and we want to share them with you in the hope that you don't make the same mistakes when you face difficulties.

"That's why they say 'wise old men and women'—because wisdom comes with age," said Mai's grandmother.

Mai was listening with her eyes wide open. "It is special to grow older and gain wisdom. I look forward to the time when I am wise just like you, Grandma! You are very wise, and I learn so much from you. Thank you for letting me work with you, Grandma. I learn so much just being around you!"

EPILOGUE

Andy, Rob, Daniel, Hannah, Mai, and Isabella were sitting in front of the elementary school near the flagpole with the American flag waving proudly. They were talking about how great a school year it had been and how they had enjoyed becoming the best of friends. They were sad that the school year had ended. But, they were happy they would see each other during the summer.

"It's been such a wonderful school year with you all, my friends," Andy said.

"Yes, yes, I agree with you, Andy. We were all in the same class at the beginning of the school year in September and here we are in June the best of friends," said Mai.

"We've really become the best of friends throughout the school year! We've been to each other's houses, played sports together, studied together, volunteered together and helped teach our classmates and each other important lessons on character. I am so glad we are lifelong friends now," said Rob.

They were all smiling and laughing as they continued to talk about their year. Then an idea popped into Hannah's head.

"Hey, as we have tried to show good character this year and help teach our friends how to always do the right thing, we should start a club this summer so that we can continue to help others and always remind each other to have good character," she said.

"That's a great idea, Hannah! We should call it 'The Hero Club,'" said Andy. "We can show other kids that anyone can be a hero so long as you have good character."

They were all excited and smiling.

"The Hero Club will be the best club at Lyncrest. Let's see how many people can join our club," said Mai.

"Anyone should be able to join as long as they have good character," said Isabella.

"And, it's our responsibility to help teach our friends to be heroes," said Daniel.

"That's right," said Rob. "When we show good character, our friends will learn from us."

They all smiled and knew that this would be the beginning of many great years of friendship to come. They were proud to be the first members of the Hero Club!

AFTERWORD

One of my favorite poems is *If* by Rudyard Kipling. After learning and applying the character traits in this book, I believe that any young child can develop into a person that Rudyard Kipling describes in the poem.

I hope that your child will develop character traits described in the poem. The characteristics in the book and in the poem *If* embody the ideal of character. I hope you will be inspired by this poem, as I am each time I read it. See the following page for the poem.

If, by Rudyard Kipling

If you can keep your head when all about you
Are losing theirs and blaming it on you,
If you can trust yourself when all men doubt you,
But make allowance for their doubting too;
If you can wait and not be tired by waiting,
Or being lied about, don't deal in lies,
Or being hated, don't give way to hating,
And yet don't look too good, nor talk too wise:

If you can dream—and not make dreams your master,
If you can think—and not make thoughts your aim;
If you can meet with Triumph and Disaster
And treat those two impostors just the same;
If you can bear to hear the truth you've spoken
Twisted by knaves to make a trap for fools,
Or watch the things you gave your life to, broken,
And stoop and build 'em up with worn-out tools:

If you can make one heap of all your winnings
And risk it all on one turn of pitch-and-toss,
And lose, and start again at your beginnings
And never breathe a word about your loss;
If you can force your heart and nerve and sinew
To serve your turn long after they are gone,
And so hold on when there is nothing in you
Except the Will which says to them: "Hold on!"

If you can talk with crowds and keep your virtue,
Or walk with Kings—nor lose the common touch,
If neither foes nor loving friends can hurt you,
If all men count with you, but none too much;
If you can fill the unforgiving minute
With sixty seconds' worth of distance run,
Yours is the Earth and everything that's in it,
And—which is more—you'll be a Man, my son!

—Rudyard Kipling (1865–1936)

A FREE GIFT FOR YOU!

You can download all 53 color illustrations for each chapter of *The Hero Club*. You can tack the chapter's illustration on your refrigerator as you read and discuss each story. The illustrations will be a reminder to your child about the character trait discussed in the stories and a fun way to engage your child in conversations during dinner and throughout the week.

To download your free illustrations, go to my website: ferahozbek.com/hero

A BIG THANKS AND QUICK FAVOR!

I hope you and your child enjoyed *The Hero Club*. The time you spent with your child to help them learn and reinforce the principles of character told through the stories in the book will have a positive and lasting impact on yourselves, your family and the world. As you continue to praise your child's character, he or she will identify with the character trait and do the right thing just like the children in *The Hero Club*.

If you enjoyed reading this book and found value in the stories, please take a moment to write a short review on Amazon. I appreciate your willingness to take your time to pass on your thoughts to other readers, and it helps me reach more kids and families just like yours!

ABOUT THE AUTHOR

Ferah Ozbek is a mother, daughter, wife and retired United States Air Force judge advocate. As a military defense attorney for military members and veterans, Ferah's passion is to help heroes who have been treated unfairly by the military justice system. *The Hero Club* is the book Ferah wished she had when her children were in elementary school. Nearly two decades later, Ferah wrote *The Hero Club* with the sincere hope that the stories and lessons will help parents teach their children about character in a fun and meaningful way.

For questions or comments on *The Hero Club*, send Ferah an e-mail at ferah@ferahozbek.com and visit her website at ferahozbek.com.